Rainbow Brite™

Mixed-Up Colors

By Ellie O'Ryan

Illustration by Carol Haantz

Scholastic Reader — Level 3

ISBN 0-439-66791-7

12 11 10 9 8 7 6 5 4 3 2 1   5 6 7 8 9/0

Printed in the U.S.A.
First printing, February 2005

SCHOLASTIC INC.

New York   Toronto   London   Auckland   Sydney
Mexico City   New Delhi   Hong Kong   Buenos Aires

It was a sunny day in Rainbow Land.
Rainbow Brite and the Color Kids
were going on a picnic.

The Pits were gloomy and gray.
Murky Dismal liked it that way.
"This fog will cover Rainbow Land,"
he said to Lurky.
"Soon all will be gray!"

The fog spread and spread.
"Uh-oh," said Rainbow Brite.
"Let's go inside."

When the fog went away,
Rainbow Land wasn't gray.
The colors were all mixed up!

Red carrots?
Orange plums?
Yellow blueberries?
Green juice?
Blue bananas?
Indigo grapes?
Violet apples?

"Oh, no!" cried the Color Kids.
"Don't worry," said Rainbow Brite.
"We can fix the colors.
We just need Star Sprinkles."

"Red Star Sprinkles
for Rainbow Brite!"
said Red Butler.

"Make way for
orange Star Sprinkles!"
called LaLa Orange.

"I've got yellow
Star Sprinkles!"
Canary Yellow said.

"Green Star Sprinkles
are what we need!"
Patty O'Green giggled.

"Blue Star Sprinkles
coming through!"
yelled Buddy Blue.

"Look!" cried Indigo.
"Indigo Star Sprinkles!"

"Here are violet Star Sprinkles,"
Shy Violet said quietly.

"Thanks!" said Rainbow Brite.
She scattered the Star Sprinkles
all over.
Like magic, the colors were fixed!
"Hooray!" cheered the Color Kids.

Rainbow Brite and the Color Kids
had a great picnic.
Everyone was happy . . .

. . . except Murky and Lurky!